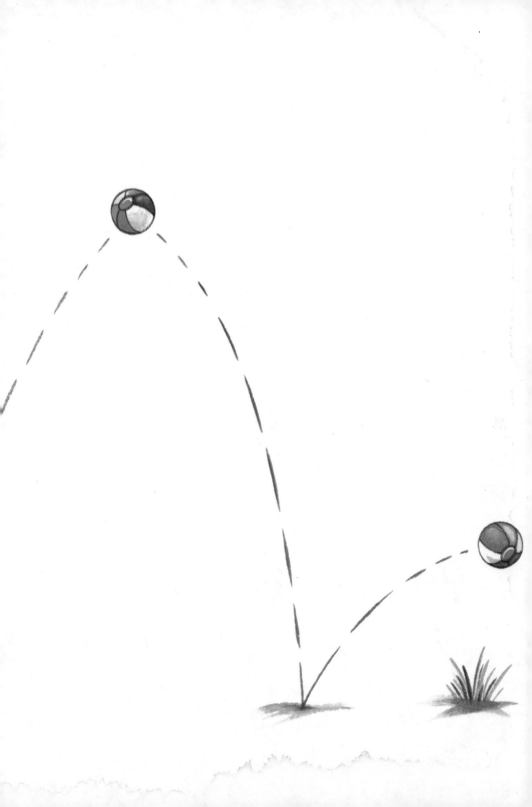

MY FIRST
I Can Read Book®

Biscuit's New Trick

story by ALYSSA SATIN CAPUCILLI
pictures by PAT SCHORIES

SCHOLASTIC INC.

New York Toronto London Auckland Sydney
Mexico City New Delhi Hong Kong Buenos Aires

ISBN 0-439-65268-5

12 11 10 9 8 7 6 5 4 3 2 1   4 5 6 7 8 9/0

Printed in the U.S.A.   23

First Scholastic printing, February 2004

For Anthony and Ruby, the newest
—A.S.C.

To Laura
—P.S.

Here, Biscuit!

Look what I have.

Woof, woof!

5

It's time to learn
a new trick, Biscuit.
Woof, woof!

It's time to learn
to fetch the ball.
Ready?

Fetch the ball, Biscuit.

Woof, woof!

Silly puppy!

Don't roll over now.

Get the ball, Biscuit.

Fetch the ball, Biscuit.

Woof, woof!

Where are you going,
Biscuit?
Woof!

11

Funny puppy!
Fetch the ball,
not your bone.

Let's try again.

Fetch the ball, Biscuit!

Woof, woof!

Good puppy!
You got the ball.
Woof!

Wait, Biscuit.

16

Bring the ball back!

Woof, woof!

Let's try one more time.

Fetch the ball, Biscuit!

Woof, woof!

Oh no!
Not in the mud!

Stop, Biscuit!
Don't fetch it now!
Woof!

Oh, Biscuit!

23

You did it!

You learned a new trick!

Woof, woof!

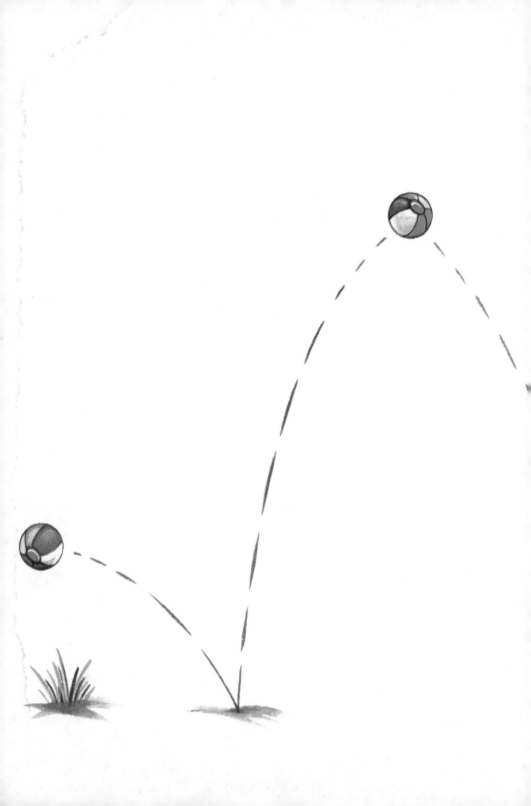